RUNNING
AWAY FROM
HOME

For Sam — N.G.
For Alexander and the Barrys — G.R.

Text copyright © 1995 by Nigel Gray. Illustrations copyright © 1995 by Gregory Rogers.

Published by Crown Publishers, Inc., a Random House company, 201 East 50th Street, New York, New York 10022

Originally published in Great Britain by Anderson Press Ltd., London, in 1995.

CROWN is a trademark of Crown Publishers, Inc.

Manufactured in Italy

Library of Congress Cataloging-in-Publication Data
Gray, Nigel.
Running away from home / story by Nigel Gray ; pictures by Gregory Rogers.
p.   cm.
Summary: Sam gets so angry at his father one day that he runs away from home, but he soon feels sad and lonely.
[1. Fathers and sons—Fiction. 2. Runaways—Fiction.] I. Rogers, Gregory, ill. II. Title.
P27. G7813Ru 1996   95-38217
[E]—dc20
ISBN 0-517-70923-6 (trade)

10 9 8 7 6 5 4 3 2 1

First American Edition

RUNNING
AWAY FROM
HOME

BY NIGEL GRAY

ILLUSTRATED BY
GREGORY ROGERS

Crown Publishers, Inc. New York

ONE SUNDAY AFTERNOON, Sam's dad was being even more mean and bossy than usual. Sam shouted, "I don't want to live with you, ever again! I'm leaving home!"

Sam went into his bedroom, got his school backpack, and dumped all his school things onto the bedroom floor.

He then stuffed into the backpack: two pairs of shorts; three T-shirts; one pair of pajama bottoms; one pair of underpants; three socks; his *Very First Poetry Book* and *Winnie the Pooh*; a few cars and play people; his recorder; a special piece of wood he had found; his flashlight (which had no batteries); some batteries (of a different size—batteries always came in handy); his treasure box with its crystals, stones, and shells; his beanbag frog; and a bag of marbles.

Sam could hardly lift the backpack off the ground. He set it down and took out the shorts and T-shirts and pajama bottoms.

Sam got his backpack onto his back. He tucked his pillow under one arm, and Low Brow under the other.

At the door he stopped, said good-bye to all his friends, looked sadly around the room that he'd lived in all his life, and went out through the living room.

He paused on his way to pet the dog. He kissed her on the head. "Good-bye, Bella," he said, trying not to cry. Bella thumped the floor with her tail and licked his hand.

"Where are you off to, ragamuffin?" Sam's dad asked.
"I'm going away and I'm never coming back!" said Sam.

Sam went out onto the veranda and let the screen door bang shut behind him. It had been raining on and off all day. Just then, it began to pour.

Sam went down the stairs and stood under the house looking out at the downpour. He was planning to live in the den that he and his big brother, Joe, had built in Whistlepipe Gulley. But it was raining cats and dogs and he didn't want to get Low Brow and his pillow wet.

The wind began to blow. The trees shimmied and shook like the grass skirts of South Sea Island dancers, and the road shone like a stream.

Sam waited for the rain to stop, but it just poured down in a torrent. The backpack was heavy and the straps were cutting into Sam's shoulders. Sam looked around for somewhere to hide until the rain stopped, and decided on Joe's skateboard ramp.

Sam watched the road for a while. Occasionally a car hissed by. He could hear a bird singing. "I don't know what you've got to sing about," Sam said. He took out his *Winnie the Pooh* book.

Sam tried to read the story about Eeyore losing his tail. But usually Sam's dad read to him, and Sam found it a difficult story to read on his own. Besides, Eeyore was so sad, and that made Sam sad too.

Sam put his book away and took out his recorder. He lay back on his pillow and played for a while, melancholy music that he made up as he went along.

Above his head he saw a brown spider in its web. Sam jiggled the web a little to give the spider a seesaw. The spider scurried off into a dark corner and disappeared.

"Come back, spider," Sam said. "Please come back." But the spider didn't come back.

"Now I've got nobody," Sam said.

Suddenly the downpour eased
off into a drizzle. Sam decided
it was time to go. He repacked
his backpack, hoisted it onto
his back, picked up his pillow
and Low Brow—and then
remembered something he'd
forgotten.

He went back up to the house.

"Hi, Sam," said Dad.

"Have you come home, dear?" asked Mom.

"No!" said Sam. Bella jumped up and wagged her tail and licked his arm.

He went to the bathroom and got his new toothbrush (the one shaped like a lady's leg that Joe had given him for Christmas) and slipped it into the pillowcase.

"Would you like a piece of cake before you go?" Dad asked.

"No!" said Sam.

"You don't have to leave home if you don't want to," Mom said.

"I want to," said Sam.

Sam went out onto the veranda. He stood for a while watching the gentle rain washing the world clean. The wind had subsided and the trees had stopped their wild dance. He turned around and went back in.

"I think I will have the piece of cake," he said.

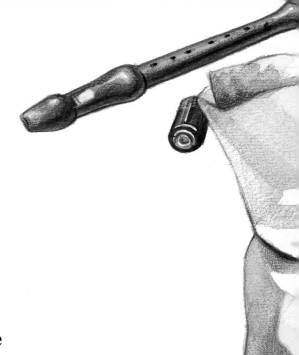

He dumped his things on the floor.
The *Winnie the Pooh* book slid out of
the backpack onto the rug. Mom gave
him a glass of orange juice and a large
slice of carrot cake.

"Do you want me to read you a story?"
Dad asked.
"Okay," said Sam.
"Do you want to sit on my lap?" Dad
asked.
"No," said Sam.

So Sam lay on the rug and heard about how Eeyore lost his tail but then found it again. Bella came to sit beside Sam and she gave his face a lick.

"She's telling you she's glad you're here," Dad said. "And I'm glad you're here too."

"All right," said Sam. "I'll give you one last chance."

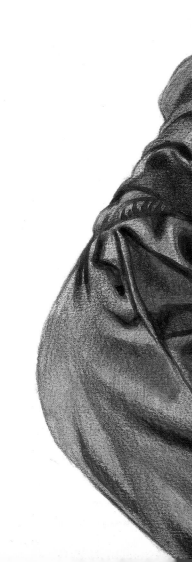